MW00914938

Lydia's Gift

To Alexandra ♡

Kimberly K. Schmidt ~

Lydia's Gift

ADVENTURES AT GRAYSON FARM

Kimberly K. Schmidt

Illustrated by Marina Saumell

Copyright 2017 Kimberly K. Schmidt
All rights reserved.

ISBN-13: 9781540456946
ISBN-10: 1540456943
Library of Congress Control Number: 2016919298
CreateSpace Independent Publishing Platform
North Charleston, South Carolina

Published by Barnyard Press, USA

Visit us at www.kimberlykbooks.com

Illustrated by Marina Saumell
www.marimell.com

This is the simple principle of the spiritual life:
The most privileged access of grace is through
our greatest weakness.

Anonymous

To the real Lydia, who inspired this story.

Table of Contents

CHAPTER 1

The Birth

~

BONNIE PACED RESTLESSLY IN HER stall. The pain was getting worse. She spooked at a loud clap of thunder and flash of lightning as it flickered in the dark sky. The storm raged outside and lit up the stall briefly, showing a calico cat with yellow eyes nestled in the corner, watching her horse friend closely.

Pacing and pawing in the straw, the mare broke into a light sweat. A wave of pain hit her hard and fast. She lowered herself into the deeply bedded straw, her great belly dragging her down as she fell with a grunt. She stretched herself full length on the floor of the stall. Her eyes glazed over in concentration; her body tightened, and her back legs, rigid, stretched out behind her. Suddenly, gallons of water gushed from her as two small feet and a nose appeared from under her tail, encased in a glistening bubble.

An occasional grunt was the only sound as she strained and pushed with all her great strength. Then, in minutes, as quickly as it had started, it was over. And there in the straw lay the result of all her efforts: a beautiful chestnut foal.

CHAPTER 2

Mr. and Mrs. Little

~

"I CAN'T STAY LONG," SAID Mrs. Little to her sleepy husband, who entered the comfortable farmhouse kitchen tying the belt of his robe.

Yawning, he ran his fingers through his thick, rumpled gray hair and adjusted his wire-rimmed glasses. "How is the foal-watch going?" he asked. He peered into the old stone fireplace and used the poker to coax the hot coals back to life.

"She was comfortable and munching hay when I left. But you know how sneaky Bonnie can be. She'll wait until I leave to have that baby," she responded as the teapot whistled. She poured a cup of tea to fight off sleep.

Rubbing his eyes, Mr. Little said, "I heard something on the news tonight about a horse-theft ring. Thousands of dollars' worth of tack has been stolen—and several valuable horses too. The bad news is that Cedar Creek Farm was hit."

"Oh no! Not Brad Johnson's place?" Mrs. Little asked, slowly setting down her cup.

"Yes," Mr. Little said. "I called him as soon as I heard the report on the news. Unfortunately, they got away. The police think they've left the state and headed north."

"Well, I hope they catch them soon," she said as a shiver ran down her spine. "At least they aren't in Virginia anymore, but if they come here, Jake and Bella may have something to say about it— right, guys?" Resting on their beds by the fire, the ever-alert dogs lifted their heads and pricked their ears toward their mistress's voice. She walked over to stroke the sleek black heads and scratch the silky ears of the two matching Dobermans.

"I better get back to the barn. I think tonight is the night," she said as she slipped on her old, stained barn coat and green rubber boots. Carelessly tucking loose strands of her short blond hair with beginning streaks of gray under her floppy rain hat, she grabbed a few clean, dry towels and headed out the kitchen door. The petite figure in the oversized coat and hat gave the competent farmwoman a vulnerable appearance as she headed into the stormy night, splashing through the puddles on her way to the barn.

CHAPTER 3

The Unexpected

~

"ALL LOOKS WELL, MY FRIEND," purred Puzzle the calico cat from her cozy bed in the hay manger. Puzzle's immaculate coat was a patchwork of black and white and orange with a perfect white bib and four white paws. She was very proud of her white bib and paws and cleaned them meticulously. Puzzle pricked her ears at the soft sound of approaching footsteps crunching in the gravel. The stall door creaked as Mrs. Little opened it slowly and peered inside.

"Bonnie, you did it again! It looks like you don't need me at all," said Mrs. Little to the tired mare lying in the straw with her wet newborn. Noticing the cat nestled in the corner, she said, "Oh, hello, Puzzle. Always the faithful friend, I see."

Blinking her yellow eyes slowly, Puzzle yawned and began a low rumbling purr, opening and closing her paws as she continued to keep watch over her friend.

Mrs. Little approached the foal quietly. "Hello, little one," she said softly, reaching out to stroke the newborn. "I've been waiting for you."

Bonnie rested in the straw, still exhausted from her labor and delivery. Focused on her baby, her ears pricked forward and nostrils fluttering, she nickered softly to the foal. As if from an electric shock, the baby startled at the first sound of its mother's voice. The foal pointed its ears toward the sound and lifted its tiny muzzle. A high-pitched whinny filled the still night from its quivering nostrils and open mouth, shaking the foal's small body and bringing tears to the experienced horsewoman's eyes. She had witnessed many births, but this moment of recognition between mother and baby never failed to move her.

A retired nurse, Mrs. Little prided herself in not letting her emotions get in the way of any medical care. There was much to do and still a long night ahead of her. She busied herself with the tasks at hand. First she put iodine on the short remnant of the umbilical cord. Then she rubbed the shivering foal with thick, warm towels until dry. Only then did she check for the sex of the baby.

"A filly!" she said, pleased. "Hello, Lydia! I've had your name picked out for you, just waiting. You're such a beautiful girl. And so big and strong!"

The filly was lying in the straw while her mother stood over her and licked her dry, inhaling her scent and memorizing her smell. Her dark, wet coat was drying, and a shiny, coppery red was taking its place. Her short flaxen-blond tail flipped and twitched. She looked around curiously, her neck waving about unsteadily and her ears floppy with the looseness of a newborn. But the urge to nurse was strong even now.

"You are a strong one," Mrs. Little said as the filly struggled to get her long legs under her. Driven by instinct to stand and nurse, she stretched out her front legs first; then, pushing with her hind-quarters, she heaved herself up for an instant. She wobbled sideways, struggling to keep her balance. In spite of her efforts, her front legs crossed, and down she went in a heap.

"Don't worry. You'll get it, girl," Mrs. Little said, laughing softly at the filly now lying in a heap on the bed of straw, legs all askew.

That's when she saw it. Mrs. Little saw what Bonnie and Puzzle already knew. All her nurse's training came flooding to the front of her brain. Her heart sank as she looked at the beautiful, healthy filly, innocent with newness, her head held high on her unsteady neck and ears swiveling forward and then backward, taking in all the sounds of her new world. Alert and curious, she looked at Mrs. Little with her still-unfocused vision. From her *one eye.* Where her left eye should have been was an empty socket lined with soft reddish eyelashes — blinking, but seeing nothing.

CHAPTER 4

Weaning Day

~⌇

"I DON'T THINK I'M READY, Mother," said the tall, leggy filly standing behind the large, dark-chestnut mare. She leaned against her mother's flank and stuck her head under the long tail, unsuccessfully trying to hide. "Can't we wait longer?" she asked.

Bonnie looked at her beautiful daughter, remembering all her past babies and how they feared this day, and knew Lydia would adjust quickly. "It's time. You'll be fine, and I won't be far away."

Calmly standing beside her nervous daughter next to their cheerful red barn, Bonnie gazed across the nursery paddock thick with tall grass to the adjoining weaning field. A horse's snort carried on the fog, sounding much closer than it was. Birds twittered and sang joyously in their ritual welcome of another morning. Sergeant Pepper, the old rooster, crowed loudly from the chicken yard, arrogantly claiming the barnyard as his own. Bay and chestnut, black and gray, the horses grazed in pairs in their pastures fenced in oak boards painted white. Bonnie turned from the scene in front of her and faced her daughter.

"Lydia, the day has come. You're ready. I've taught you all I can. The rest is for you to discover and learn on your own. Remember the rules of the herd and to follow them, always. Before long, you will be grown, and Mrs. Little will be teaching you how to be a riding horse—and maybe someday, even a show horse."

Lydia lifted her head proudly at the thought of being a show horse. Then she saw Mrs. Little approaching holding a new leather halter with a shiny brass nameplate and a lead rope in her hand. Her newly found courage evaporated. Pawing the soft earth with her front hoof, Lydia shook her head and snorted nervously. "I'm not going. It's scary over there. The gate is too narrow. I don't want to go through it." Having exhausted all her excuses, she planted her feet firmly, refusing to budge. Mrs. Little gently tugged on her lead as Bonnie calmly led the way through the gate.

"Time to be weaned, girl. You'll be fine," the kindly woman said, giving the weanling a gentle pat as she turned and brought her mother back inside the mare paddock and closed the gate behind her, separating Lydia from her mother for the first time.

Bonnie walked across the paddock to where the other mares were grazing. Her friend Rosie whinnied, welcoming her back to the mare herd. Lydia called to her mother, lonely and forlorn. Bonnie nickered encouragement.

"Your mom is right here on the other side of the fence, so she's not far away—you can talk to her. But no more nursing, I'm afraid. Grain and grass for you now, little one," said Mrs. Little. "You'll be fine. I promise you." She smiled sympathetically.

CHAPTER 5

Introductions

~

"MOTHER?" LYDIA CALLED OVER THE fence in a high-pitched whinny. She anxiously watched as some young horses approached her. She was nervous and didn't know what to do. Relieved, she saw a young colt she recognized.

"It'll be okay, Lydia," called her mother. "Just sniff noses. These kids aren't much older than you, so you'll be fine. And of course, you know Samson. You just stay with him for a while." Bonnie continued to graze with the other mares, glancing over at Lydia every so often to make sure she was doing all right.

Lydia gathered her courage. "Maybe this won't be so bad. It will be nice to have friends. We can run and play. Maybe it *is* going to be okay," she told herself hopefully.

"Come on, Lydia. You can graze with me," said Samson, an attractive dark-bay colt with a perfect white stripe on his face.

Lydia and Samson were the only two foals born that year. They had both been together in the nursery for the last six months with their mothers until Samson was weaned one week before Lydia.

"I'll introduce you to the others," Samson said, leading her over to the two yearling fillies in the herd. "Sally and Maddie, this is Lydia."

"Hi," said Lydia shyly. The fillies were so pretty. Sally was gray, almost silver in color, and had the prettiest dapples. Maddie, a bright-red bay, was very shiny and had four perfectly matched white stockings.

Sally sniffed Lydia's nose but gave her an odd look and said to Maddie, her best friend, "Let's go over to graze at the big patch of clover." The yearling fillies walked away, side by side, whispering and looking back at Lydia.

Lydia started to speak to a beautiful large black colt, but he walked away without saying a word.

"That was Caesar," said Samson in a low voice. "Caesar is two years old and will be leaving the weaning field at the end of the summer to go to the big barn to start his training." Samson was clearly in awe of the herd leader, a striking black colt with a small star as the only marking on his glossy black coat. Caesar walked away, head held high, clearly aware of his rank as number one in the herd.

CHAPTER 6
Mean Girls

~

"COME ON, GIRLS, IT'S BEEN almost a week now. You've hardly spoken to her. You can cut her some slack. You're fillies, after all, so you should be the ones to take her into your group," said Samson. "Here she comes. Be nice!"

Maddie said in a low voice, "It's kind of sad, really. What will Mrs. Little ever do with her, I wonder?"

"Who knows," said Sally, uninterested, tossing her silvery mane.

"I feel badly for her; she'll never be a show horse," said Maddie.

"She might be a pleasure horse, I suppose, but that will be all," said Sally. "She most certainly will never be able to jump. I love to jump. Any limb that blows in the field, I practice jumping over. I want to be a famous jumper when I grow up and go to Madison Square Garden like my mama did," said the vain gray filly.

"Shhh," said Samson. "She's coming." Samson watched her approach. "Hi, Lydia. I can't talk now. I'm on my way to hang out with Caesar awhile. Guy stuff, you know," said Samson.

"Oh, really?" said Sally teasing. "*You* and Caesar are hanging out now. Ha!"

"We are too," said Samson, stung by her insinuation that he wasn't good enough for Caesar. "Caesar is older, and he's teaching me stuff. He's so cool!" he said, excited about his new friendship with the oldest and number one horse in the Order. "Caesar is going to be a dressage horse when Mrs. Little starts his training. He has big, fancy gaits and practices trotting around the field, arching his neck and rounding his back so that it looks like he's floating across the field. He's showing me how to move like he does. He thinks I have talent," he said proudly.

Sally snorted a laugh into Maddie's mane.

"Lydia, you can hang out with the girls," said Samson, glaring at Sally. "See you later," he said, trying not to notice Lydia's miserable expression as he galloped across the field to where Caesar was grazing.

CHAPTER 7

Zack and Mack

~

WATCH OUT BELOW!" CAWED THE two black crows, Zack and Mack, in unison as they dove at the red-tailed hawk that was soaring over the barnyard looking for an easy meal among the pecking chickens. Hearing the crow's loud warning, the panicked chickens scattered for cover. The tormented hawk finally flew off in disgust to find an easier meal elsewhere.

"Well done, my friend," said Zack to Mack, tucking his wings as he flew, dipping and swooping and rolling effortlessly.

"Show off." Mack laughed at the acrobatics of his friend.

"Look," said Zack, suddenly doing a beautiful stall mid-swoop. "There's that nice young filly, Lydia."

"All alone again, I see," said Mack.

"Hello," they said together as they prepared to land upon the oak fence next to where she was grazing. They almost always spoke in unison or finished each other's sentences. It made for a most confusing and loud conversation.

"Oh, hi," Lydia said glumly.

"Why so sad?" asked Zack. Flapping his wings expertly, Zack slowed his descent and settled on the fence, light as a feather. Mack followed Zack's example and was all set for a perfect landing. Then, without warning, he made a quick detour and, diving low, plucked a shiny silver treasure stuck on a briar. Spreading his wings, he swooped up and did a snappy landing on the fence next to Zack.

"Let me see!" demanded Zack. "What is it? Something shiny, I hope," he said, stepping closer as he snatched with his strong black beak at the object hanging from Mack's beak.

"Oh no you don't! Quit being so grabby. It's a treasure I found for our collection!" said Mack proudly. "It's probably made of real silver," he said of the shiny gum wrapper he had found.

"It's beautiful," said Zack admiringly, hopping from one foot to the other excitedly.

Holding her breath, trying not to laugh, Lydia finally couldn't hold it in any longer. "I don't mean to laugh at you, but you don't know how you just cheered me up. That's the first good laugh I've had in a long time!"

"We're always glad to cheer you up, Lydia. We'll show you our treasure collection sometime if you'd like," they said together, their words tripping over each other.

"Oh, I'd love that! Nobody else seems to want to share anything with me. Even their time," she said sadly.

"What's up?" asked Zack, concerned for the young filly. "What can we do to help?"

"Oh, nothing, I guess. I just get tired of always being left out. Only Samson will talk to me, and sometimes I think he just does that to be nice. Maddie and Sally are best friends, and now Caesar and Samson have paired off. That leaves me all alone, and none of them will let me join them. I don't know why," she said, looking down and scratching slow circles in the dirt with her hoof.

She brightened as a thought occurred to her. Turning suddenly to the crows, her thick flaxen forelock lifted off her face, revealing her missing eye. Zack and Mack exchanged glances but continued preening their black glossy feathers and listening politely.

Lydia's words all tumbled out in a rush. "Do *you* know why they won't be friends with me? I don't get it. I always follow the herd rules. I'm nice, and I have a pretty red coat and a flaxen-blond tail. I'm tall, and I can run fast. Do you know why they won't be my friend?" She paused and asked slowly, "Is something wrong with me?"

"Umm, of course not. Nothing is wrong with you," said Zack uncomfortably.

"In fact," said Mack, nudging Zack in the ribs, "I think you may be better than the others, but they just don't know it."

"Oh, sure," said Lydia, her head drooping again. Peering at them from under her forelock, she said, "Wait—you really mean it!"

"Sure," said Mack. "We can teach you stuff that they don't know. You probably already know a little but don't realize it."

Lydia held her head a little higher. "Tell me."

"When we fly, not only does the wind lift us from under our wings, but we can also feel the shifts in the wind's directions and tell when storms are coming. We'll teach you how to feel the wind. The wind can tell you lots of things."

"Okay," said Lydia, willing to give it a try.

So Zack and Mack told Lydia all about how the wind shifts direction before a storm, how the pressure in the air changes, and how electrical charges fill the air just before a bolt of lightning appears. They taught her how to tell the difference between the feel of a thunderstorm and when a tornado is about to form. They taught her how to tell when a blizzard is coming and predict how bad it would be—all just by feeling the wind.

"Be sure to practice, and we'll be around if you need us," said Mack.

"Speaking of wind, something is blowing across the field," said Zack, his wings lifting him into the air.

"Wait for me. Where is it?" asked Mack.

"Oh no you don't," replied Zack. "This one is mine, and it's bright red! Probably a valuable jewel," he said as they raced each other to the treasure rolling across the grass.

CHAPTER 8

A New Skill

~

"SAMSON, GUESS WHAT!" EXCLAIMED LYDIA when he came to the run-in shed for dinner that evening. They always ate from buckets hanging side by side on the fence.

"What?" asked Samson, gobbling his food down as fast as he could. He was always hungry. He was growing at a rapid rate and looked like he might make a muscled dressage horse after all. He wanted to be just like Caesar.

"Zack and Mack taught me all about the wind today," said Lydia, hoping to impress her friend.

"Listen, Lydia. You don't want to be seen talking with crows. They are good to warn the smaller animals about predators with their loud caws, but they're beneath us horses. They collect trash, you know. Nasty! You'll never be allowed to be in the inner circle of the herd if you're seen talking with crows."

"Why? I don't get it. Besides, they make me laugh. And they're nice to me," she said with a pout.

"Just do as I say," insisted Samson. "I'm trying to convince the fillies to let you join their pair and make it a threesome. They're not ready yet, but I'm working on them. Don't mess it up," he said with one last lick of his bucket. Turning his back, he walked away, leaving Lydia alone. Again.

CHAPTER 9
Jake and Bella

~

"OH DEAR," SAID BELLA TO Jake as they saw Lydia standing alone in the corner of the field, head down and tail slowly swishing at flies.

"Poor dear," said Bella. "It's so sad about her, um, disability, you know. Poor thing. How will she ever manage in this world?"

"Humph. You're too soft with the young ones," said Jake as they continued their walk around the farm. "The child needs to know the ways of the real world. Needs to toughen up. No need to coddle her. Well, since we're here, I guess we might as well talk to her. It would be impolite, otherwise," said Jake, gruffly.

"Oh, you don't fool me for one minute, Jake," said Bella, giving him a gentle nudge with her nose as they approached the lonely filly

"Hello, Lydia. We were on patrol and thought we'd take a short break," said Jake as he lifted his head and sniffed the air in all directions.

"Don't worry about him, dear. He never really takes a break. He's always on the job. But tell me: How have you been? You seem a little down. What could be bothering you on such a beautiful day?" asked Bella.

"I'm all right, I guess," said Lydia, hanging her head.

"What is it? Can we help?" Bella asked, tilting her beautiful, chiseled head and silky ears and looking at the sad filly with her sharp, intelligent gaze.

"I haven't made any friends, so I've been trying to learn some new things so that maybe the other horses will like me. I've been practicing feeling the wind for approaching weather. The crows are teaching me. I'm not very good at it yet, but I think I'm learning. I know I notice more than the other horses. But then, in some ways, I think I always have. It's funny in a way. They don't seem to know what I'm talking about sometimes."

"Well," said Bella, looking at Jake and carefully choosing her words. "Maybe they don't understand what you're saying because you're more special than they are."

"What do you mean?" Lydia asked, perplexed. "I'm not special."

"Never mind," Jake said quickly.

"I know what!" said Bella, changing the subject. "Why don't we teach you something too? You know, like Mack and Zack did."

"Yes!" said Jake, catching on. "A wonderful idea." He nodded at Bella. "And it has something to do with the wind, so it will be easy for you to pick up. It has to do with the breeze. And smelling scents in the air. Of course, we smell scents on the ground too, but you will most likely pick up more on the breeze, as tall as you are. Dogs smell thousands of times better than humans," Jake said proudly. "We hear much better too. So, what do you say? Do we have a plan?"

"I think it's a perfect plan!" said Bella enthusiastically. "We can teach you to hear and smell better than the other horses! They'll be so impressed. Then surely they will let you be friends."

"That sounds like it just might work!" said Lydia hopefully.

"We might as well start right now," said the motherly dog, feeling badly for the lonely filly. "Now, pay attention. Do you feel that breeze?"

"Yes. Mack and Zack taught me to always be aware of any breeze," Lydia said.

"That's right. The breeze brings more than the weather to you. It also brings you sounds and smells," explained Bella.

So Jake and Bella taught Lydia all about turning her face into the wind so the wind would bring the scents to her nose and how to open her nostrils wide and lift her head and point her nose into the breeze.

"A fox has a very strong scent, so it's easy to smell. I once heard Mrs. Little say that even humans can smell a fox. I'm always amazed at how poorly humans can smell," Jake mused. "I don't know how they survive. Good thing Mr. and Mrs. Little have us to watch after them. But never mind. Your first lesson will be a fox scent," suggested Jake.

"I have an idea!" said Lydia. "Every morning Red and Vixen trot across the back of our field on their way to scout out the hen house. They always trot by just as the sun is coming up."

"That sounds perfect," said Bella. "We'll meet you right here at dawn tomorrow morning."

"Yes. And be on time!" said Jake sternly. "I don't want to be kept waiting. I have other things to do, you know. You have a lot to learn, young lady. I expect you to practice."

"Oh, I will, Jake. I promise," said Lydia nodding at him solemnly over her shoulder as she walked away.

"No coddling, did you say? You old softy. You don't fool me for a minute. You'll have this child scenting as well as one of your pups." Bella pushed Jake gently.

"Humph. Don't be ridiculous. Softy, indeed. Humph," he said, trying his best to frown seriously. "Back on patrol, my dear." He glanced over at Lydia, wrinkling his brow with concern as she went in search of a friend.

CHAPTER 10

The Eager Student

~⁓

As PLANNED, JAKE AND BELLA arrived at dawn. Lydia was already there, waiting for them eagerly.

"Oh, good. Here you are!" said Lydia. "I got up early to make sure I wasn't late."

"Let's get started with our lesson, then," said Jake, already proud of his young student. "The sun is almost up."

Lydia lifted her muzzle into the air, sniffing the scent on the wind blowing toward her from the far end of the field. She immediately picked up an unmistakable musky odor.

"There it is!" she said. She smelled the fox before she saw him trotting across the field in the distance.

"That's it," said Jake. "You've got it! You are certainly a fast learner. Almost as good as a pup. Now all you have to do is practice getting downwind and sniffing. Pretty soon you'll identify all kinds of smells. Humans, cats, skunks— Oh! By the way: keep away from skunks! And you should practice smelling coyotes as well as foxes. Learn the difference. And watch out for the coyotes. Alone, one would not be a problem. But they can be dangerous in a pack. Call us if you ever smell any of them." Growling under his breath, he said, "We'll take care of those rascals if they come around."

"Stop it, Jake! You'll scare her," said Bella. She turned to Lydia. "You'll also smell the hay when it's cut and the rain after it's fallen. It's a lovely world, you know, the world of smells," she said, shaking her head in warning at Jake.

"Breezes will also carry sounds from great distances. Nothing special to do there except to practice listening and pay attention all the time. Always be alert. And take advantage of those wonderful big ears of yours   1 all directions. They will catch all kinds of sounds,' said Jake.

"Okay," said Lydia. "Funny, but it seems I already hear things before the others in the herd do. But I will practice that too."

"I'm not surprised your hearing is better than the others, dear," said Bella before Jake could give her a nudge to be quiet. "Oh, right," said Bella. "We'll be off now, dear. We'll stop by tomorrow."

"Thanks, Jake and Bella. I can't wait to tell Samson," she said as she went in search of her childhood friend across the field.

~

"Hi, Samson. There you are. Guess what! I'm learning something new!" she called excitedly as she cantered over to tell Samson all about her new lesson.

"Lydia. I'm worried about you. You need to be more careful who you hang out with. No more crows, I hope. I told you not to talk to them anymore," Samson said.

"Well, they are my friends, so I do talk to them," she answered, lifting her head in defiance. "But no, that's not what I am talking about. I talked to Jake and Bella. This morning they taught me all about picking up scents and sounds on the breeze. Did you know that everything has its own smell? And if you practice, you can get really good at smelling things far away. And hearing, too. I found out I can hear really well!"

"Lydia," said Samson with a snort, "really, you shouldn't spend time with the dogs, either. You know that coyotes and wolves are natural enemies of horses. Well, dogs are not much different. At least the other horses will think so, anyway. You're never going to be accepted into the herd if you don't quit talking to those that are beneath us. I'll talk to the fillies again. But you have to help me out."

"Don't you even want to know what I learned?" asked Lydia slowly. She had been so excited to share with her childhood friend.

"As far as I can tell, all I need to smell is the grass and grain and water and hay under my nose," he answered as he ended the conversation, turned his back, and trotted over to Caesar, leaving Lydia behind.

CHAPTER 11

Puzzle

~

"IT'S SO WONDERFUL TO TAKE naps in the sun, don't you think?" said Puzzle to Lydia, more of a statement than a question. Yawning and stretching her supple feline frame, she awakened from her second nap of the morning.

"I suppose so," said Lydia, grazing alone, waiting her turn at the water tank. "See all the others in line to drink?" she asked. "I even have to wait for Samson to finish now. He's not mean, exactly—just a little proud. He won't let me drink with him side by side anymore, like he used to. I'm only allowed to drink after the others have finished. I'm last in the Order," she said sadly.

"What's 'the Order'?" asked Puzzle, walking along the tightrope fence effortlessly and admiring her skills immensely.

"My mother explained it to me. In horse society, there is a hierarchy, or order, from first to last. The horse who is first is always the herd leader. Usually it is the oldest, most mature horse. It goes on from there, one after the other, until the last. Somebody has to be in charge, and that is Caesar in our herd. I'm just tired of always being last even though Mother warned me that the youngest would usually be last. But not for long, she said. I thought Samson was my friend, but he talks to me less and less. I swear, they all act like something is wrong with me, but I can't figure it out," said Lydia.

"Oh, don't worry about them," said the friendly cat. "I think having friends of your own species is overrated anyway. Personally, I like being the only cat in the barn. It is all my kingdom, and that suits me just fine," she said, jumping off the fence and rolling in the dust, turning her belly up to the sunshine. Suddenly, without warning, she jumped up and scampered off with her tail in the air, bristled like a bottlebrush, as if she had just been startled.

"What was that? Did something frighten you?" exclaimed Lydia. "Oh my! One minute you were lying down, and the next, you were dashing away! You are very quick!"

"Yes, I know," purred the conceited cat. "I *am* very quick," she said, rubbing around and between Lydia's legs.

Lydia stood very still so as not to accidentally step on the affectionate cat.

"You know," purred Puzzle, "I don't like other cats much, but I have always liked horses. It's funny, I guess, but my mama was the same way. She even had us kittens in a hay manger in the mare barn. Dogs I can tolerate if they have manners like Jake and Bella, but I prefer not to share my barn with other cats. I just like horses. That's all there is to it. And your mother is particularly special to me, dear. As you know, I was there for your birth," said Puzzle, remembering that day as she glanced quickly at Lydia's missing eye.

"That's fine for you, maybe, but not for a horse," explained Lydia. "Horses are herd animals, and it's just natural for us to want to be with other horses. My mother taught me all about herd etiquette when I was just a little foal, and I always do what she said and mind my manners with the herd. But they still don't like me."

Perking up, she said, "At least the crows and dogs have been nice to me. They taught me some new things. They taught me how to feel the wind and determine the weather coming and how to smell a scent and hear a sound on the breeze—not that those are things a show horse really needs to know, but it has been fun to learn anyway. And it was kind of easy for me to learn, actually. I don't know why. Oh well. At least it's something to do by myself."

"Well, I can teach you something too," said the indignant cat. "I certainly can teach you more than a dumb dog and a silly bird."

"What can *you* teach me, Puzzle?" asked Lydia.

"I can do something that those dogs and crows cannot do. And I am going to teach you. Ha! We'll show them!"

"What?" asked the curious filly.

"I can see in the dark!" Puzzle announced proudly. "And I am going to show you how!"

"Wow! I didn't know anyone could see in the dark really well, other than owls!"

"Bah! Cats are much better than owls," said Puzzle, not knowing if that was true but wanting to impress her friend. "Okay, let's get started. Tonight, when the sun goes down and darkness is here, I will come and meet you by the gate."

CHAPTER 12

Cat Eyes

~

"OKAY, NOW, THE FIRST THING you need to learn to do is to open the pupils of your eyes very wide," said Puzzle to Lydia as the sky slowly darkened into night.

"You mean *eye*. Horses only use one eye for seeing."

"Right, that's what I meant," said the flustered cat. "Eye."

"You won't be able to open your pupils—I mean, *pupil*—as wide as mine because cats' pupils are slits and special for seeing in the dark. They open very wide, while yours are round and can't open as wide.

But you can still learn to see at your best. Now, concentrate on that twisted oak tree over there by the fence. See if you can find the broken limb hanging down near the top," said Puzzle.

"I can't see it," said the frustrated Lydia as the twilight faded into darkness and the moon started to rise. She wanted to get it right the first time.

"Just wait. It will come. Keep concentrating," said the ever-patient cat.

"There it is! I can see it now. It's coming into focus slowly. Wow!"

"Now you just need to practice every night so you get accustomed to controlling the pupils of your eyes—I mean, *eye*—and you will be able to see in the dark better than all the other horses."

"Thanks, Puzzle! I *will* practice!" said the excited Lydia, thinking of her new skill and how surely this would impress the other horses.

CHAPTER 13

No Time for Lydia

~

"SAMSON, GUESS WHAT!" SAID LYDIA excitedly.

"What is it now, Lydia?" said Samson, sounding irritated. "Sorry, but I don't have much time to talk. Caesar and I are going to practice our *piaffe*. That's a fancy dressage movement," he said, puffing out his chest. "Caesar is teaching me how to move like a dressage horse. He said a good dressage horse has a big, bouncy trot, and looks like he floats across the ground," he said proudly. "This is important, so I need to go," he said as he turned to leave.

"Wait! I want to tell you something," said Lydia.

"What is it? Tell me quickly. I really have to go," he said, looking over his shoulder in Caesar's direction.

"Puzzle taught me how to see better in the dark! Isn't that cool?" said the filly hurriedly before Samson could run off. She hoped that Samson would finally be impressed.

"Well, if you had to talk to someone besides a horse, at least it was a cat. All horses like cats, so that's okay. But it's still not going to help your low place in the Order. And seeing in the dark is not really something you need. Humans ride horses in daylight or in a lighted ring. But then you may never be ridden, anyway," he muttered this last to himself.

"What do you mean? Never be ridden! Of course I'll be ridden. And I *am* going to be a dressage horse too, Mr. Smarty Pants!" Lydia huffed angrily. "Why would you say such a thing? That was mean!"

"Oops! Sorry, Lydia. I didn't mean anything by it. Got to go. See you later!" And he trotted off quickly to find Caesar for their evening practice session before it got too dark.

CHAPTER 14

The Secret

~

LYDIA HEARD THE CLIP-CLOP OF horse hooves and looked up from grazing to see her mother approaching with Mrs. Little astride.

"Hello, dear," nickered Bonnie, as she and Mrs. Little came to a stop in front of the weaning field. "Mrs. Little and I are going for a ride to check all the fence lines. I need to keep in shape, you know," she said, arching her neck and sucking in her belly.

"How's my special girl?" said Mrs. Little to Lydia as the tall filly stretched her long, elegant neck over the fence and nuzzled her mother. "You are growing up to be a beauty! Before too long, it will be time to start your training."

"Ha! Did you hear that, Mother? ! I will too be ridden!" snorted Lydia in a huff.

"Of course you will, my dear," said her mother, nodding her head. "Tell me, how are you doing? Have you made a best friend yet?"

"Mother, nobody will be my friend," replied Lydia. "They act like something is wrong with me, but they won't tell me. They whisper and look at me, and even Samson is not friendly anymore. He even said I would never be ridden! What did he mean, Mother? Why would he say that?"

"Well, honey, I guess you are old enough for me to tell you. I never thought of you as disabled— and you certainly never acted like it— so I decided to just let it go and not say anything. Maybe that was wrong of me. But have you noticed how the other horses have two eyes?"

"Yes. So what? I do too. One I see with…and the other one…"

"Yes, dear. But your other one is actually missing, and you have only eyelashes around where the eye should be."

"What do you mean?" asked Lydia with a sinking feeling.

"The other horses can see out of two eyes. You can see out of one. You're blind on one side."

"What do you mean, blind?" said Lydia, disbelieving. "I can see you just fine! And I can see the other horses way up on the top of the hill," she said, not realizing she was tilting her head slightly to the side in order to increase the field of vision for her good eye.

"It doesn't matter, honey. Don't you worry. Mrs. Little has always said you are going to make her a wonderful dressage horse, and she wants to keep you for herself and will never sell you. You can do everything the other dressage horses can do. I promise. Are you all right?" she asked as Lydia gave a big sigh and hung her head.

"Yes," said Lydia in a soft voice. Thanks for telling me, Mother. Now a lot of things are starting to make sense."

"Let's go, girl." Mrs. Little nudged Bonnie forward with her heels. "Enough nuzzling your baby. We're running out of daylight, and clouds are moving this way." They headed off to enjoy the last light of the summer evening. Glancing back, Bonnie saw Lydia staring at her reflection in the water tank, as if seeing herself for the first time.

CHAPTER 15

Beware

~

MRS. LITTLE URGED BONNIE INTO a trot and then a slow canter. She smiled as she felt the wind in her face and the rocking motion of the horse under her as they cantered across the hayfield and approached a trail leading into the woods. Without warning, Bonnie spooked hard with a snort, stopped quickly, and spun around, ready to bolt.

"Whoa, girl! What's the matter?" said Mrs. Little to the nervous mare, adjusting the loosened helmet on her head. Looking around, she didn't see any obvious reason for the spook—other than the fact that it had gotten dark faster than she realized.

"Must have been a shadow, I guess." She shrugged. "Better take a shortcut through the woods, girl, or we won't get back before dark. Come on now." She stroked the sweaty neck of the prancing mare as she turned her into the darkening shadows.

∼

"Hello, dear. Did you have a nice ride?" asked Mr. Little as his wife came into the kitchen, shedding her muck boots and rain slicker.

"It was lovely, except Bonnie was spookier than usual. I don't know why. You know how steady she usually is. I couldn't see any reason for her behavior. Then a nasty drizzle started up when we were about halfway through our ride. When we got back to the barn, I gave everyone a warm bath to clean off the mud. I put on their mesh sheets and gave them each a flake of alfalfa hay to munch on until they dried off. Bonnie especially enjoyed her spa day after her nervous, sweaty ride. That was so unlike her. Very odd," she said in a puzzled voice. "I've never seen her so eager to get back to the barn. She usually loves our long rides."

"I wondered why you were later than usual," said Mr. Little. "I know how you like to watch the news and weather every day, so I recorded it for you."

"Thank you, dear," Mrs. Little said, as she pulled on some dry clothes—an oversized sweatshirt and some thick wool socks — before snuggling on the sofa to watch the news. "Listen!" Mrs. Little exclaimed, sitting upright. "They saw a mountain lion at a farm not too far from here. It killed some of their lambs! I didn't know we even had mountain lions here. Certainly not this far east! They are rarely seen at all, and then only farther west in the mountains. Certainly never here in the lowlands."

"Oh, it was probably just a bobcat and someone overreacted," assured her husband, as he put on the teapot to boil.

"I don't know," said Mrs. Little. "They sounded pretty sure on the news. If a big cat comes around here, hopefully the loud barking of the dogs will make it think twice about coming too close. I hope so, anyway. Jake certainly likes to make his presence known," she said as she looked affectionately at her two dogs resting on their beds, and hoped they would not be in danger as well. She knew they would not hesitate to protect any person or animal on their farm.

CHAPTER 16
A Bad Feeling

~

"I WONDER WHAT THAT SMELL is," said Lydia to Puzzle, who was sleeping on a pile of hay in the corner of the cozy shelter, avoiding the rain. Puzzle hated to get wet and appreciated the horses' cozy, dry barns and shelters. Lydia ate her hay, nibbling around the dozing cat who was not bothered at all by the meal being consumed around her. Lydia lifted her face and pointed her muzzle into the breeze that had just picked up.

"I've never smelled that before. What do you think, Puzzle?"

"Smelling long distances is not my thing. You know that, Lydia. I like the short-distance smells like mice and baby birds and baby rabbits. Yum, yum!" she said, licking her lips.

"Oh, yuck! No, really. I smell something new. And I have a feeling it's bad."

"You seem to always have a feeling. Maybe it's nothing this time. It's probably just something the buzzards are eating on," said Puzzle, licking her perfectly white paws. She insisted on always being spotless. She was especially vain about her white paws and bib around her throat and chest.

"Something is really wrong. I just know it," insisted Lydia nervously. "Oh, look, here comes Mrs. Little with our evening grain. Maybe she will notice something."

"Dinnertime!" announced Mrs. Little cheerfully, as the other horses trotted up for their meal. "Oh,

Puzzle, there you are," she said as she picked up the purring cat. "I'll take you back to the big barn so you can sleep in the hayloft. It's going to get really nasty tonight. We're expecting a thunderstorm.

"Lydia, what's the matter with you?" she murmured to the obviously nervous filly, stroking her neck to calm her. "You're not acting like yourself," said Mrs. Little. She moved her hands over the filly, feeling for any injury, and found nothing. She checked her pulse and respirations. She carried a thermometer in her pocket at meal times, just in case she needed to check a sick horse.

"No fever," she said, talking out loud to herself. "Hmm. Your pulse is a little elevated, and so are your respirations, but just slightly. I don't think it's anything to worry about. I guess it's nothing. Probably just tired of this wet, nasty weather. Don't worry, girl. Tomorrow is supposed to be sunny and warm after this front moves through. But I'll check back on you later, if I can, just to make sure."

Mrs. Little gave each of the young horses a scoop of grain in their personal buckets and walked back to the barn, carrying Puzzle and scratching her behind her ears as her purrs got louder.

CHAPTER 17

The Truth

~

"SAMSON. TELL ME WHAT IT'S like when *you* see," Lydia blurted out.

"What do you mean?" asked Samson nervously, eating faster from his bucket. Mealtime was the only time anymore that he and Lydia were alone to talk.

"Don't worry. Mother told me. She said I was blind in one eye. Is that why the other horses won't be my friend?" she asked sadly.

"Yeeees, maybe," he said slowly, looking at her out of the corner of his eye, shifting his weight from side to side, suddenly uncomfortable.

"Tell me what it's like for you. I want to know how you see differently from me. I can see. I don't see what the big deal is," she said.

"Okay, Lydia," said Samson warily. "I'll try to answer your questions. What do you want to know?"

"Tell me what it's like for you to see."

"Well," he said, taking a deep breath, "as you may have noticed, horses' eyes are at the sides of our heads. Slightly toward the front but not straight in front like dogs and cats and people."

"Now that you mention it, you are right. Go on," insisted Lydia, determined to learn all she could about this.

"So, since our eyes are more on the sides of our heads, we can see almost all the way around us. A little bit straight behind us we can't see, and a tiny bit straight in front, but other than that, we can see all around us. That's so we can see anything scary or dangerous from all sides. We just have to turn out heads slightly to the side, and we can see behind us. No need to turn all the way around. That way, we can take off and run in an instant. Very few animals can sneak up on us. Only birds overhead, I guess, but they are not a danger anyway. Do you understand now?" asked Samson, uncomfortable.

"Yes," Lydia said, swiveling her head from side to side, for the first time noticing how limited her field of vision was. "I can see everything on the right side of my body and partway behind me, just like you said. But I don't see anything on the left side." She was astonished that she had never thought that his was odd before. She noticed how she turned and tilted her head to see better things in the distance.

"How do you manage?" asked Samson, carefully.

"What do you mean?" asked Lydia.

"How do you know if anything is on your blind side? Sometimes you even sleep on the ground with your good eye facing down and your blind side facing upward. It seems like you would always be careful to have your good eye up so that you could see. I have always wondered about that."

"I don't know," said Lydia. "I guess I am so used to it that I never knew my way of seeing was any different than everyone else. So I have never thought about it. But also, I can just tell when something or someone is next to me on that side."

"What does that mean?" snorted Samson, unbelieving and thinking maybe Lydia was lying to make herself feel better.

"I don't know," wondered Lydia. "I can just tell when someone is coming up on my dark side. That's what I always called it, anyway. My dark side and my light side. I can just feel it. If Mrs. Little walks up to me while I am lying down and strokes my neck on my dark side, I know she is going to touch me before she does it. I can just tell. I feel her getting closer. I just know she is there."

She paused, struggling for the right words. "I feel her presence. I don't know how to explain it."

"I don't believe it," said Samson. "No offense, but you probably just hear her coming up to you."

"Maybe," said Lydia. "I do notice that I hear things before the rest of you do. For that matter, I smell things first too. But I think that's something different."

"I don't think you can hear or smell better than me!" said Samson. "There's nothing wrong with my ears or nose! You are just trying to make yourself feel better. Humph!" he said as he turned and trotted off. He was going to tell Caesar what Lydia had said. Caesar was the oldest of them. He would know what to make of this.

CHAPTER 18

The Storm

~

LIFTING HER NOSE INTO THE wind, Lydia felt nervous. Something was wrong. They were all grazing far from their shelter, way down at the distant end of the field. Their field was an old hayfield, so there were no trees in it—lots of grass, but no trees. Lydia knew this was good because during a storm, a horse could be struck by lightning when taking shelter under a tree. Lydia had heard horror stories about that. But no trees also meant no shelter from pelting rain and driving winds. Of course, Lydia knew that standing on top of a bare hill could be just as dangerous as under a tree. And, right now, they were at the highest place in their field. They were the tallest things in that field, which made them vulnerable to lightning strikes.

"We should go!" Lydia urged the others.

"Whatever for?" asked Maddie. "So much wonderful green grass, and finally a wind has picked up to cool us off."

"I agree," said Sally as a gust of wind lifted her silky mane off her hot neck. "Oooh...that felt wonderful!

"Really, guys! I think we should head back to the run-in shed. I think a storm is coming," urged Lydia.

"So what?" said Caesar. "I'll be the one to decide when we move, anyway. Not you!" He glared at her, surprised at her rudeness and lack of herd etiquette.

"Something is wrong! I can feel it!" said Lydia, starting to fidget.

"There you go again. She can just *feel* it!" Samson said, being unusually mean to his childhood friend. Lydia knew he was still stinging from her earlier remark about him not hearing as well as her.

Suddenly a gust of wind, stronger than the others, sprang up. The temperature seemed to be drop quickly. A few big drops of rain started to fall.

"Well, maybe we'll move a little closer, just in case it starts raining hard," said Caesar, casually. Lydia knew he was proud of being head of the herd. But she also believed Caesar was a good horse and truly wanted to be a good leader and would do what was best for his herd. She let out a long sigh, trying to be patient and let Caesar be the leader.

"We can walk back to the shed, now. But no need to rush. It's just a little rain. Besides, it will feel good after such a warm day," said Caesar.

Caesar heard a distant rumble and glanced up at the sky briefly with a worried look on his face. But decided the sound was too far away to be of immediate concern.

Lydia was happy they were moving in the right direction, but she was getting more and more nervous. She always seemed to be more aware of her surroundings than the other horses, and she had been practicing her new skills from the crows on feeling incoming weather on the wind.

Lydia lifted her nose into the wind. Now she knew for sure. Alarmed, she said insistently, "Guys. It's going to hail! We need to run. This is going to be bad!"

"Hail! You've never seen hail in your life, and neither have I," snorted Samson with a shake of his mane. "You and I were born the same spring. How would *you* know? Just trying to get attention, that's all. Humph!"

"The crows taught me. And I can just tell," said Lydia insistently, not knowing what else to say. She didn't care if they were mad at her. She knew something bad was going to happen.

"Ha!" said Caesar, insulted. He *was* the leader after all. "So now we listen to crows. Bah! All they are good for is being an alarm— warning about nearby fox and hawks. And I couldn't care less if a fox or hawk is around. So their opinion means nothing to me!"

The young herd had made it about halfway down the long field. They were still a long way from their shelter when the first hail started to fall. First it began with small, marble-sized pieces mixed in with the increasingly pelting rain. It was turning very cold, very quickly.

"Ouch! That hurt," said Sally, who was a bit prissy anyway.

"Okay, everybody, time to trot in to the shelter, just in case this gets worse. No need to panic, though. Follow me," said Caesar, still keeping control of his herd.

Lydia knew better than to pass Caesar. As herd leader, he was always in the front. She was supposed to be last, but she was impatient, running back and forth from back to front, trying to get the others to hurry up.

Then it happened. Golf ball–sized chunks of ice fell from the sky. Like a shot, the whole herd took off in a full gallop, manes and tales streaming, nostrils closed and ears flattened against their heads to keep out the rain, ducking their heads from the rock-sized blows.

Just as they all skidded into the shelter, crowding close to let everyone in, the hail began pummeling the metal roof with tennis ball–sized pieces.

Lightning cracked around them, and thunder boomed. All the horses crowded close, shivering in the strange cold air in the middle of August.

The storm raged most of the night. Trees fell in the woods, and a power line fell over the fence, sparking and hissing before going silent. The horses did not sleep. They snorted occasionally and waited nervously until the storm passed. Finally, there was silence. Then came the sound of tree frogs chirping in the thickets.

CHAPTER 19

A Near Miss

~

THE DAY DAWNED WITH A clear blue sky and air that smelled washed clean. The sound of birds was the same as any other summer morning. The five young horses, slowly and carefully, began to peer outside the shelter to see what had happened to their world during the night. There was a large fallen tree lying over the fence, split in two by a lightning strike. A splash of red among the fallen branches was a dead cardinal. A downed power line was sparking and jumping on the ground not too far from the shelter. The horses were silent at first. None of them said anything to Lydia.

"Lucky guess. That's what I think," muttered Sally to Maddie. "Of course she could tell a storm was coming. All of us could. No big deal."

"But she did know first, and she did say it was going to hail," said Maddie, hesitantly giving Lydia credit for sounding the first warning, just beginning to realize the danger they had been in had Lydia not alerted them in time.

"Just lucky, I say," insisted the arrogant Sally. "She's half-blind, for heaven's sake! There's no way she could know more than us. And certainly not more than Caesar," said Sally, admiring the black gelding, who was more mature than the other young horses. Caesar was not saying anything.

Lydia looked around at all the horses. She had hoped that by helping the herd, it would make a difference and they would finally accept her. But it had not. She pretended not to hear Sally's mean words.

"At least we got to the shelter in time," Lydia murmured to anyone who would listen as she munched on the hay slowly. "I have heard stories of horses struck by lightning. They die instantly, my mother said. They are dead before they hit the ground."

They all shivered. They too had heard the stories and knew what could have happened had they not reached their shelter in time.

CHAPTER 20

Mountain Lion

~

SHIVERS RAN DOWN LYDIA'S SPINE. She stopped and lifted her nose into the breeze, opening her nostrils and taking deep breaths. The sun was setting low over the trees, but it was not yet completely dark. Two weeks had gone by since the storm. Lydia had tried not to mention it, as it seemed to irritate the others, especially Samson. She tried not to say anything at all. But now something was wrong. She knew it. She had felt it for hours, but now she had to say something.

"Samson." Lydia spoke in a low voice. "I smell something different. I don't know what it is, but I know it's bad. I feel it. Help me warn the others. They'll listen to you."

"Stop it, Lydia! Quit trying to scare everybody," said Samson. "You and your feelings. Always trying to show off. No wonder you don't have any friends," snorted Samson as he turned back to eating a particularly nice patch of clover he had found. The herd was slowly moving down the field on a clear starlit summer night, grazing as they went.

There was a flicker of motion in the trees on the other side of the fence.

"Caesar. Look! Warn the others! Something's in the trees!" said Lydia, desperately trying to get the herd leader to listen to her.

"All right, Lydia," Caesar said, trying to be a good leader and be patient. "Where do you see something?"

"Over there by the willow tree."

"I don't see anything. It's too dark over there." Caesar was beginning to get a little irritated, and just as he turned his back to leave, Lydia spooked so hard she jumped sideways and whinnied a high-pitched cry of terror.

"There, it's coming!" she said in despair.

Then Caesar saw it. "Run, run, everyone!" Caesar said as he caught the flicker of motion under the willow tree just as a very large cat bounded over the top of the fence, touching the top rail lightly and sailing over. The mountain lion flicked its tail as it landed softly in the grass. It was heading straight toward the grazing horses, slinking through the tall grass, flattened to the ground and ears pinned back on its head.

"Run!" said Caesar again. The frightened horses took off in a gallop. All were following Caesar, automatically looking to their leader for guidance. With necks stretched out, nostrils flared and ears flat-tened, they ran for their lives.

The lion was getting closer. The horses were approaching the end of the field near their run-in shed. But the shed was no shelter from a mountain lion.

"Get ready. We have no choice. Follow me," said Caesar as he gathered himself to jump the five-foot-high board fence. Just as he planted his feet to push off the ground, one hind foot slipped in the mud. He managed to get off the ground but hit the top board, breaking it in two and ripping it off the fence posts, leaving nails exposed.

The others follow Caesar, jumping the now-lowered fence with the top rail down. Lydia, last of all, was unsure of herself. Now that she knew of her blindness, she didn't know if she could jump. She had never jumped before. Maybe she would not see properly and fall and be eaten by the lion.

"Shhh," she said to herself. "I can't think about that now." And over she went, her front legs folded in perfect form, clearing the fence easily.

CHAPTER 21

Run!

~

"CAW, CAW!" SAID ZACK AND Mack, who had seen everything from far overhead.

Mack began diving at the mountain lion to distract him and slow him down while Zack flew ahead to give instructions to the horses, whose instinct was telling them to run to the shelter of the big barn. But they knew that would only bring danger to the other horses, and they would all be trapped if the lion ran into the barn after them.

The panicked horses were milling about after jumping out of the field, not knowing which way to go.

The frustrated mountain lion screamed and swatted at the annoying crow, trying to grab the pesky bird with his giant paws and pull it out of the sky. With a leap and a big swipe of his paw, he snagged some feathers out of Mack's tail, who dodged and ducked just in time.

"Run to the house! Follow me!" cawed Zack. "Mrs. Little will help you."

Zack led the way, flying just in front of Caesar down the lane to the farmhouse. They had no other plan, so they followed Zack. They were fighting to control their panic and were thankful for any guidance.

"My goodness!" exclaimed Mrs. Little as she and Mr. Little stepped out onto the back porch when they heard the pounding hooves. "What is going on? How did you get out? Whoa, kids! It's all right. Whoa," she said in a low voice, calming them down.

"What has gotten into you?" she said, concerned. Her eyes scanned them for injuries as they all stood there, shaking and blowing.

Stroking Caesar's neck, she noticed the gash on his chest. "Not too bad, but looks like you will need a few stitches. Let's get that cleaned up and call the vet," she said calmly as she led the nervous, sweaty horse back to the barn with the others following closely behind.

"What a racket those crows are making!" exclaimed Mrs. Little. The early evening sky was lit with a full moon. She gazed toward the edge of the woods, where the crows were cawing, and she could just barely see them diving and swooping, obviously upset about something.

"Maybe it's a fox they are mad about," she said. "But my, I don't think I've ever heard them fuss so much."

"And what's the matter with you two?" said Mrs. Little to Bella and Jake, who had come out of the house on her heels. Low growls erupted deep in their throats as their hackles raised down their backs. They took off to the edge of the woods, where the crows had been, and stopped abruptly. Standing with stiff legs, heads raised and barking a warning into the woods, they watched and listened to the disappearing crows moving further in the distance, still cawing and diving.

Walking over to the field to survey the damage, Mr. Little said, "I'll fix the broken fence now before they decide to jump out again," and he went to gather his hammer and nails.

Mrs. Little made a decision. "Come on, Caesar. I need to clean that wound of yours, and then you are going to sleep in the barn tonight. I hope you learned from your foolishness not to try to jump a five-foot fence! For goodness' sake—you're not even three years old yet, and you think you can jump the moon! You're going to be a dressage horse, anyway, so you can just stop that nonsense right now!" She shook her head, wondering what had gotten into him. "In fact, you might as well stay in the barn from now on. I was going to bring you up to the big barn for training in a few months, anyway. We'll just start your training a little early, is all— once your wound is healed," she said fondly, stroking the big black colt.

CHAPTER 22

No Leader

~

BACK IN THEIR FIELD, WITH fence repaired and gate locked, the other young horses looked at each other in despair as they saw Caesar being led away and into the barn. "Oh no! What will we do without Caesar?" wailed Sally and Maddie. "Without him, we won't know what to do! What if that monster comes back?"

Panting, Jake and Bella came trotting back from the woods, where they had been exploring and sniffing. Ignoring the frightened Sally and Maddie, Jake got right down to business. "Tell us what happened," he said to Lydia. "And what did we just smell? I've never smelled anything like that before."

"It smelled sort of like a bobcat," said Bella, "but different somehow."

"It was a mountain lion," said Lydia, shivering.

"A mountain lion!" said Jake. "I've never heard of one coming this far from the mountains. But don't you worry. We'll keep watch tonight. Bella and I will take turns."

"Thanks. I don't think any of us will sleep a wink tonight," said Lydia, and for once, the other horses nodded in agreement with her. But they would not speak to the dogs. Caesar had told them that dogs were beneath them and not to speak to them. They were glad that Lydia would talk to them, but they would not admit it. They were scared and felt better with the dogs guarding them that night.

～

"Dear. You'll never guess what I just heard!" said Mr. Little to his wife as she entered the kitchen early the next morning. "Jerry called from across the road at Gallant Hill Farm. It seems he saw a big cat sneaking into his cow barn early this morning. It killed a calf before he could shoot it. It got away, but at least it's gone now. He thinks he scared it off. He saw it running across Highway 20 heading west toward the mountains. Thank goodness it ran off before it came over here and got one of the horses."

"Oh, no! " Mrs. Little said, having a sudden thought. "I wonder if that's what the dogs were so upset about last night. I wonder how close we came to having a tragedy ourselves. I don't even want to think about it," she said as a shiver ran down her spine.

CHAPTER 23
Stranger Danger

~

SALLY TIPPED HER HEAD FROM side to side, admiring her reflection in the water tank.

"I can't wait for the horse show this weekend," she said with one last admiring look. "Mrs. Little is giving me a bath today. I love baths! The water is so warm, and I look so pretty after a bath, you know. Any stains left in my white coat will be gone, and the gray dapples will show up so nicely. And my mane and tail will be braided very fancy. Mrs. Little thinks I will win first place," said Sally with a toss of her head.

Samson rolled his eyes at the vain gray filly.

"That's nice, Sally," said Lydia sadly. She knew she would never be in a conformation class because of her missing eye. The conformation class was a beauty show for horses. Only the most beautiful horses were entered.

Suddenly, Lydia noticed something odd over by the barns. "Hey! Look at those men. Something is wrong there," said Lydia, noticing the two strangers for the first time. The two men were dressed in dirty clothes and looked slyly from side to side before taking a show flyer off the bulletin board at the main barn. With one last backward glance, they got into their truck and drove off. "I'm glad they left. They gave me a weird feeling," said Lydia.

"Oh, you and your feelings," said Sally, still admiring her own reflection in the water tank.

CHAPTER 24

Horse Show

~

SHOW DAY ARRIVED, AND THE young horses gathered at their gate, watching eagerly as all the horse trailers arrived at Grayson Farm for the annual Hanoverian Breed Show. It was a well-known show, and breeders from all over Virginia brought their young horses in hopes of winning first prize in their category. Also, interested buyers came to see the new crop of young horses and hopefully find that one special horse to buy.

The concession stand was selling coffee and doughnuts and breakfast sandwiches. Children were holding onto their parents' hands as they walked down the stall aisles looking at the well-groomed horses with polished hooves and braided manes. Sally and Caesar were entered in the show, so they were in the main barn in order to stay clean and for spectators to admire.

"Look!" said Lydia, her ears pricked in the direction of the parking area. "There are those two strange men again," she said with a bad feeling. They were in dirty farm clothes and did not seem to be with any of the competitors. They did not have children with them and were not watching the show at all.

One of the men was short, with slicked-back dirty-blond hair. His small eyes darted back and forth as he scratched his stubbly chin. He leaned over and whispered to the taller man in overalls and a flannel shirt walking beside him. He was tall and thin with a beaked nose and thin lips and wore a slouchy hat.

Lydia wished she could hear what they were saying, but they were too far away. She saw them wander into the main barn, where Caesar and Sally and the other horses were, who were entered in the show that day.

"Look, there's Mrs. Little! Surely she'll see those strange men and ask them to leave."

Mrs. Little was busy with the entries and getting the judges started with their first class. There were lots of spectators milling about the concession stand. Mrs. Little did not notice two more people. She was busy, and there was too much going on.

But Lydia noticed them. She had a bad feeling. "Look, here they come!" said Lydia to Samson and Maddie.

"Oh, look! They are bringing carrots for us. Lydia, you must be wrong," said Maddie, who especially loved treats.

The men wandered from paddock to paddock until they came to the gate to the weaning field past the barnyard. The short man with little eyes reached his hand out to give Lydia a carrot.

"Ouch! She bit me!" he said as Lydia pinned her ears, and, missing the carrot entirely, bit the man hard on the fingers.

"And look, Horace. I think something is wrong with her eye," he said as Lydia turned her hind end to him and kicked, hitting the fence with a loud crack.

"Ha-ha!" laughed the tall, thin man at his friend. "Otis, I think horses just don't like you. Watch me. This one is nice," he said as he fed carrots to Maddie, who happily took the treats.

"Stop it, Maddie!" said Lydia sharply. "Don't eat those!"

"Mind your own business," said Maddie, gobbling as many carrots as she could as the man gave some to Samson too.

"Let's go," said Otis angrily, rubbing his pinched fingers. "That lady over there is watching us. We better go."

"Good-bye for now, my pretty little horses. We'll see you later," said Horace as he gave Maddie and Samson one last treat.

"Besides, we still need to check out the tack rooms," said Otis, giving the horses a disdainful look.

The two men walked off and disappeared into a crowd of happy spectators.

Mrs. Little had seen the two men give carrots to the youngsters. She didn't like it when people fed her horses treats. They usually meant well, but they might give them something unhealthy. She was glad to see them leave and turned back to handing out programs and entry numbers to the competitors.

"I wonder what he meant, that he'd see us later?" said Lydia as she shook her head and stomped her foot.

"Too bad Mrs. Little leaves Jake and Bella at the house during shows. I know they wouldn't like them either," said the agitated filly.

"Quit worrying, Lydia," said Samson. "Maddie is right. If you keep worrying, you are going to miss out on all the fun. You didn't even get one carrot."

CHAPTER 25
Horse Thieves

~

"YOU SHOULD HAVE SEEN ME!" said Sally to her friends at the end of the day. She was happily looking at the blue ribbon that Mrs. Little had hung on the front of their shed.

"I won the yearling class, and Caesar won the two-year-old class! Mrs. Little was very proud of us," said Sally, telling the others all about the show.

"That's nice, Sally," said the others, who were happy for her but who were also very tired of her bragging.

They were exhausted from the busy day and settled down to sleep early.

"What's that I hear?" said Lydia suddenly, rousing herself from her sleep. The moon was full that night and the sky was clear with an occasional cloud floating by. There was a little breeze that Lydia felt in her face.

"Shhh. I'm tired," said Sally, who was always grumpy if awakened.

Lydia sniffed the breeze and focused on dilating her pupil like Puzzle had taught her so that she could see in the minimal light. The first thing that hit her was their smell.

"It's those bad men!" she said in alarm.

"What bad men?" asked Samson. "Go back to sleep."

"The bad men who came and fed you carrots during the show. It's them; I can smell them!" she said.

"Look! There! I can see them now. They are pushing wheelbarrows out of the big barn down the lane to the road. How strange. It looks like saddles in the wheelbarrows."

"Where?" said the others, now fully awake.

"I don't see anything," said Samson, still irritated with Lydia for waking him up.

"Oh!" said Maddie excitedly. "Look, it's those nice men with carrots. Maybe they are bringing more."

The youngsters watched as the men returned from down the lane with now-empty wheelbarrows. The men stopped and turned, looking toward the weaning field. Speaking in low, raspy voices, they approached the horses with carrots held out in one hand and halters and lead ropes behind their backs. Lydia could smell their smoky breath as they got closer.

CHAPTER 26

Taken

~

"HELLO, MY PRETTY LITTLE HORSES! Remember me? I have more treats for you!" said the tall man named Horace, holding a carrot in his hand.

All the young horses strained their necks over the fence to get the yummy carrots they remembered from earlier that day. All except for Lydia.

"Let's leave the mean one," said Otis, rubbing his fingers from the memory of being nipped by Lydia. "I thought I saw something wrong with her eye anyhow."

"Okay by me. But we take the others," said Horace as he attached a lead rope to each of the leather halters the horses wore. "Come on, sweet-ies. I have apples too this time. All cut into juicy pieces." The horses stretched their necks for the sweet apples.

"Otis, you get the colt, and I'll bring the gray and bay fillies. We'll leave the chestnut one. We don't need her," said, Horace who seemed to be in charge.

Otis took Samson's lead and gave him a juicy piece of apple. The tall man led Sally and Maddie together. Sally had missed out on the treats earlier and was thrilled to get some now. Maddie had told her all about these nice men.

"Don't go!" whinnied Lydia, as she stomped her feet and pinned her ears. She reared, pawing the air and shook her head. "Something's wrong. Stop, stop! Don't go!" The men had forgotten to close the gate. Or probably didn't care. It swung open.

"Come on, Lydia. You'll see; it's all right," said Samson as he followed the nice man with the apple pieces. "You don't want to miss out again. Besides, they are pulling on our ropes, and Mrs. Little taught us that means to follow."

The three youngsters obediently followed the men who had hold of their lead ropes. Lydia, not knowing what else to do, followed at a safe distance.

The two men led them through the barnyard and down the lane toward the gravel road at the back farm entrance. The young horses had never been this far from their field before. There were trees closing in on each side of the drive. They could hear the distant sound of highway traffic.

"I don't know," said Sally, who was not as brave as she liked to pretend. "This is kind of scary. Maybe we should listen to Lydia this one time," she said a little nervously.

"I think so too," said Maddie in a shaky voice, slowing down as the man pulled harder and harder on her lead rope.

All the horses came to a complete halt as they saw a big stock trailer parked just outside the farm gate.

"Get out the bags, and put them over their heads," said Horace. He wanted to get out of there. "They'll follow us if they can't see. That always works."

"Here. Hold these three. I'm going to get the one who is following. Even if she does have a bad eye, we can always sell her by the pound, if you know what I mean!"

"Ha-ha! Good idea." Otis laughed.

Lydia had already decided she was not leaving her friends. So she stood quietly while the tall man put on a halter and lead rope and the bag over her head.

Lydia could tell what was happening as well as she could have with two eyes. She sniffed the air and listened carefully. She knew these were bad people, but she would not leave her friends. She followed the others reluctantly onto the horse trailer, the last one on.

The ropes were taken off, and they were turned loose in the trailer as the back door clanged shut. They managed to shake the bags off their heads as the trailer pulled away. They spread their legs and lowered their heads to keep their balance on the bumpy dirt road. They could see through the slats, the road whizzing by.

They were frightened and didn't know what to do. The clouds had covered the moon, and the night was totally black. Lydia was thinking, but she couldn't come up with any ideas. She tried to pay attention to smells and sounds as they traveled in case it came in handy later.

They traveled for what seemed like a long time to the frightened and confused horses.

"Oh, finally, we're stopping," said Sally. "My legs are tired."

Stopping at a truck stop, Horace and Otis got out to stretch their legs and fill the truck with gas. "Let's get something to eat while we're here," said Otis. "I'm hungry." Once it was full, he put the cap back on the gas tank, and they walked inside the truck stop diner.

"Look," said Maddie. "Here come some people. Maybe they have food or water," she said hopefully.

CHAPTER 27

Thank Heaven for Little Girls

~

"Look, Mommy! Horses!" said a small red-haired girl in pink overalls, pointing at the horse trailer. "Mommy, hold me up!" said the little girl, not quite able to reach the velvety noses stretching out to her.

"Okay, honey, but be careful," said the mother as she picked the child up and held her so she could see better. Watching closely, she saw that the horses were gentle, their ears pricked forward, nuzzling the little girl's fingers softly.

A man's loud voice was heard from across the parking lot.

"What was that, Joe? I can't hear you," the mother called back to a man walking out of the truck stop diner. "Just a minute! Joline wants to pet the horses." She looked over at her husband as he walked impatiently over to their car, taking his keys from his pocket.

"Hurry up!" he called. "Time to get on the road."

"Just a minute, I said. We're coming! For heaven's sake, be patient," the mother replied, shaking her head.

The little girl petted Samson's soft nose but then noticed something else interesting. There was a metal latch with a bright yellow handle. She liked yellow. She reached over and pulled on the yellow handle. The handle turned. The door creaked.

"Time to go, honey. Your daddy is waiting on us to get back on the road."

"But Mama," said the little girl, as she saw the door with the yellow handle move slightly.

"No buts, little lady. You have petted enough horses for one day. No arguing, or you don't get the candy I bought for you." She marched off, carrying the little girl, who pointed at the trailer, but said nothing as the trailer door creaked open.

CHAPTER 28

The Escape

~

"COME ON! LET'S GO. HERE'S our chance!" said Lydia urgently.

The others were confused and scared, but Lydia had heard the scraping of the latch as it turned against the metal. Then she felt the air moving through the slight gap at the back gate of the trailer.

Lydia saw her chance and gave the gate a good shove. It swung open all the way.

"Quickly—follow me." Even though Lydia was not their leader, without Caesar, they did not know what to do. "No time to waste. They will come back soon," she said as she stepped down out of the trailer onto the parking lot.

"Come on," said Samson, "maybe it's time we listened to Lydia."

Lydia gave her old friend a grateful look as the other horses all jumped off the back of the trailer, milling about in confusion.

"This way. Follow me!" said Lydia as she led them away from the trailer and toward the road. Then they heard loud voices behind them.

"Horace! There go our horses," exclaimed the thief, just then coming out of the truck stop diner.

"Dang it, Otis, I told you to check that back gate!" said Horace angrily, as he ran and grabbed the lead ropes from the back of the truck.

"It's not my fault!" argued Otis.

"Faster!" said Lydia as they started trotting down the side of the road, cars whizzing by and horns honking.

Lydia could feel the other horses' panic as the bright lights of the cars distracted and confused them.

"Quickly! Get off the road and follow me," urged Lydia as she found a deer trail leading off the road and down a hill to a creek. "Hurry! This way," she said.

"Ouch!" said Sally, stumbling over a rock on the trail. "I can't see! It's too dark! Slow down!" said the frightened filly.

"Sorry, I forgot you can't see in the dark so well." said Lydia. "But we have to move faster than a walk. I don't trust those bad men."

Sure enough, they heard the sound of the engine of a four-wheeler coming behind them. It was coming fast.

"Hear that?" said Lydia. "That noise! They're coming!"

"I hear it!" said Samson. "Keep together, guys. Don't fall behind. What do you want us to do now, Lydia?"

They all turned and looked to her for guidance. They had no idea what to do.

"Okay, everyone. You all have to trust me and follow me. Do exactly what I say. I will tell you what is ahead. Follow my instructions. We have to run fast, though. Stay together. Let's go."

Galloping up a hill, Lydia called out, "Small log next to the big tree! Up and over!" The others could see only a shadow but trusted Lydia and jumped where she said.

"Careful, now! The trail drops off steeply at the top of the hill; there's a big gray rock on the right." One after the other, as they approached a large rock shining in the hazy moonlight, they lowered their haunches to prepare and were surprised at the steep descent. They slid to the bottom of the hill, hind ends tucked and front legs stuck out straight in front of them, keeping them from somersaulting.

"Do you smell the fox?" she asked.

"What are you talking about?" whined Sally, who was getting tired. "I don't smell anything."

"The fox has a strong musky smell. Turn right at the strong scent. That's where his den is. Be careful not to step in it. It's a deep hole," she warned them.

Turning right at the fox den, they entered a small grassy meadow about half a mile from the road.

"We'll rest here for a bit. I think we're safe now. I need to see where the farm is."

"What does she mean *see* where the farm is?" whispered Sally. "I hope she hasn't led us farther from home."

"Be quiet," said Samson. "I trust Lydia. Maybe it's time we all did."

"Come," said Lydia, sniffing the air. "There is some water over to the left if any of you are thirsty."

"How do you know that?" asked Maddie incredulously.

"I can smell it, and I can hear a trickling sound of water over rocks," said Lydia.

"Well, I don't hear anything," said the amazed Maddie, but she followed Lydia's directions. She was hot and sweaty and very thirsty. "Hey! Here it is! A nice little brook. Come on, Sally," she said to her mud-splattered friend, who was lagging behind, exhausted. "A little farther. Keep coming. See, Sally. Here it is. Lovely, clean water. Mmmm. I was so thirsty," said Maddie.

"Now all I want to do is sleep," said the unusually quiet Sally.

CHAPTER 29

Lost

⁓

LYDIA WATCHED THE SUN RISING over the distant hori-
zon. She had been awake for hours, taking advantage of the quiet and stillness. She needed to think.
She couldn't smell her way home, and she couldn't
hear her way home. And she certainly couldn't see
her way home. She needed to come up with a plan.
The others had started to count on her and she
didn't want to let them down. But the truth was,
she didn't know the way home. She was just as lost
as the others. Her goal last night had been to get
away from the bad men and then to find water and
a place to rest.

She didn't think they were too far from the farm now. They had not been on the trailer for very long. But she didn't really know how far they had gone before they escaped.

Lydia thought and thought. Then her mother's words came to her. "Always trust your feelings, dear. You know more than you realize. Trust yourself, and let your feelings guide you. They will never fail you." She closed her eyes and forgot about the sounds of the morning and smell of the mist rising off the meadow. She just tried to listen to her feelings.

Lydia opened her eye and sniffed the air in all directions. The others started to wake up and stretch.

"Which way do we go, Lydia?" asked Maddie and Sally in unison. "We want to go home," they said, completely forgetting that Lydia was younger than them and last in the Order. They were scared and hungry and wanted to be home at Grayson Farm, where they were happy and safe and cared for. They didn't like being out in the open, where bad men might find them or whizzing cars might hurt them on the roads. They missed Mrs. Little and their farm.

CHAPTER 30
Homeward Bound

~

"I HAVE AN IDEA," SAID Lydia. "I smell some freshly cut hay on the breeze coming from that way," she said as she pointed her muzzle to the east. "Mr. Little as well as our neighbors cut hay two days ago. Also, it seems fairly hilly here, and our farm is not very hilly. The mountains are to the west. So that means our farm is to the east. But other than that, I am really just guessing, guys," she admitted, wanting to be honest. "Mainly, I just have a feeling that this is the way back home."

"You and your feelings!" said Samson with a snort to Lydia. But, this time he was teasing. "Well, I for one am with Lydia," he said with a laugh, giving Lydia a friendly push. "You and your feelings have been right so far. Come on, girls. Let's follow our fearless leader!"

Lydia, happy to have Samson's confidence, took a path from the hidden meadow and headed east. The troop of young horses followed deer paths through the woods along a winding creek. They crossed many farmers' fields, but since it was a Sunday, no one was around. They kept off the roads. At some farms, small dogs ran out, yapping at them. The tired horses trudged on, heads down. They were hungry and thirsty. Night would soon be approaching.

Her head held high, Lydia tried to focus on her feelings and her sharp senses. They crossed a one-lane dirt road carefully, taking a path on the other side across a cornfield and into the woods beyond.

The unlikely troop of leggy young horses followed a bright-red filly with one eye.

Suddenly, Lydia lifted her head and said, "I think it's just over there! I can hear Jake and Bella barking far away."

"Well, I don't hear anything, but I believe you!" said Samson excitedly, straining his ears to hear the sound of barking dogs.

"Wait a minute!" exclaimed Samson. "I hear something too!"

"It's the crows, Mack and Zack! That's them cawing," said Lydia. "I can hear them getting closer."

"You mean those tiny specks in the distance?"

"Good for you!" said Lydia. "You saw them before I did. I just heard them. We'll have to count on you for your sharp eyes, Samson!"

"Caw, caw!" the crows called out loudly. "There you all are. Mrs. Little has been worried sick. The police caught the horse thieves. The owner of the truck stop was suspicious when you all escaped, so he called the police. But nobody knew where you were. Mrs. Little has been calling all the farms she knows. And Zack and I have been flying high above the farm, circling a mile wide, hoping to find you heading this way," said Mack. "Follow us. We'll lead you the rest of the way home." They both cawed loudly and happily, dipping and flipping as they flew ahead

Thankful for the lead, the tired herd walked the rest of the way, following the gleeful crows. The young horses rallied their remaining strength when they say the gate to Grayson Farm up ahead.

"Look! We're back." said Maddie, exhausted, but relieved.

Happy to be home, they broke into a trot down the farm drive and up to the big barn. Mrs. Little, hearing the clip-clops on the drive and the loud caws of the crows, stepped out of the barn into the setting sun and wiped her worried brow before she saw them.

"Oh! You're home. Thank God!" She had tears in her eyes. "Come quickly, dear!" Mrs. Little called to her husband. "They came home all by themselves. And look: Lydia is in the lead! She showed them the way," she said, reaching up to pet the beautiful face of the tired filly as she came to a stop in front of her mistress. "Lydia, my Lydia!" she said, with tears streaming unashamedly down her cheeks as she smiled and laughed and hugged her. "Come here, all of you. I need to give you all big hugs! Okay, now. Enough of this nonsense. Time to get serious," she said, wiping her face. "All of you. Time for inspection. Anybody hurt?" Mrs. Little went over the horses thoroughly. "No, you all seem okay. I know you've only been gone about twenty-four hours, but it seems like forever. How about a nice warm bran mash for all of you? Everybody gets to sleep in the barn tonight, and I'm putting a cot right here in the barn aisle too. I'm not leaving you for one minute, all night long." She opened the doors to the empty stalls in the main barn and put in more straw for extra deep bedding. "One day, these will be your stalls," she said. The youngsters admired the stalls with soft rubber mats under deep straw, automatic waterers in the corners, and a salt block above every corner feed tub.

"And, Lydia, my dear. You go to the head of the class and get the stall reserved for my best dressage horse. I know that's exactly what you're going to be one day," Mrs. Little said to Lydia. "You're absolutely perfect in every way. And don't you let anyone tell you differently!"

CHAPTER 31

School Days

~

THE YOUNGSTERS WOULD NOT START their riding education until they were nearly three years old. But they now knew there were other things they needed to learn.

"Caw, caw," said Mack to Sally. "Okay, now. Feel the breeze. Pay careful attention. Now it is southerly and warm. That means we are in for a lovely, warm day."

"Woof," said Bella to Maddie. "Lift your nose now. Sniff the air. You might need to close your eyes so that you're not distracted by what you see. Just think about smelling. Nothing else. See if you can pick up anything and if you can tell what direction it's coming from. You can do it!" she said encouragingly to her new pupil.

"Samson. I hear you have sharp vision already. You meet me right here tonight after dark, and we'll work on your night vision. It may come in handy sometime, you know," said Puzzle, laughing. "But then I guess you already knew that!"

"What I want to know," said Samson to Lydia, who was standing nearby watching the new school unfold, "is how come you figured all this out when it was under our noses all along."

"I'm not entirely sure," Lydia said slowly, "but I think it's because I couldn't see as well, so my other senses became stronger because I needed them to be. After all, half of my field of vision is totally black. And if we act like our vision is our only sense, then we miss out on a whole world of senses. Of course, my friends here helped me to use what I already had," she said, smiling at the dogs and cat and crows. "In a way, your good vision distracts you from paying attention to your other senses. Also, Bella told me that young animals have more sensitive ears than adult animals and can recognize more noises. So since we're young, it gives us an advantage over the adult horses. And of course, everything gets better with practice," Lydia stated with confidence.

"But Lydia," asked Samson, "what about those *feelings* you get?"

"Yeah, Lydia, what about those?" asked Maddie curiously.

"Oh, that! Well, that may have to be my little secret!" Lydia said, laughing.

CHAPTER 32

One Year Later

~

"LOOK! THAT'S HER. THAT'S LYDIA," whispered Donny to Molly. "She's the lead horse in this herd. She's number one in the Order! I heard that she'll start her dressage training next summer."

The new weanlings had heard stories about Lydia. Now, on their first day in the weaning field, they were meeting her for the first time.

"Oooh! I've heard about her!" said Molly. "Did you know she has only one eye?"

"Yes," Donny said, "but she has special powers. My mum told me that her senses of smell and hearing are better than all the other horses'. And she can see in the dark too. Mum told me that she has something very special. Somehow, she just knows things. That's what the older horses say, anyway."

"Do you think she'll teach us?" asked Molly. "I hear that we'll start in a special school right way. I hope so, anyway."

"Caw, caw!"

Donny and Molly startled at the loud caws as the two large crows landed on the fence, side by side, next to them.

"Well, well! Here are the new students," said Mack and Zack in unison. "Time to begin your classes, children"

"All right! Donny and Molly, is it? You have some serious lessons ahead of you. But first, you need to meet the leader of this herd and our finest pupil ever," said Zack proudly, with his head held high.

The youngsters' eyes opened wide, and they took a step back anxiously as Lydia approached to welcome the new members to the herd. Her copper-red coat was gleaming in the sun over her well-muscled body and her flaxen-blond mane lifted in the breeze.

"So these are the new weanlings. Molly and Donny, I believe?" asked Lydia.

The two friends only nodded, too afraid to speak.

"It's time to begin your studies. Don't be nervous," said Lydia to the timid youngsters huddled closely together. "You'll do fine. You have great teachers and I'm always here to help you anytime you need. Your job, with the help of your teachers, is to discover what your own gift is, make it stronger, and share it. But don't be surprised if your gift is not at all what you expected. What you thought was a weakness might actually be a strength; and your greatest gift of all."

About the Author

Kimberly K. Schmidt is a gradu-
ate of the University of Georgia
where she earned two bachelor's
degrees—one in animal science
and one in nursing.

Married with two sons, she currently lives on a farm
near Charlottesville, Virginia, where she spends
her time breeding and training horses and writing
children's books. *Lydia's Gift* is Schmidt's third book
and the second in the Adventures at Grayson Farm
series.

63202887R00109

Made in the USA
Lexington, KY
30 April 2017